# The
# Jungle Book

## RUDYARD KIPLING

STERLING CHILDREN'S BOOKS
New York

# STERLING CHILDREN'S BOOKS
New York

An Imprint of Sterling Publishing
387 Park Avenue South
New York, NY 10016

"Rikki-Tikki-Tavi Moves In"
Published 2006 by Sterling Publishing, Co.
Illustrations © 2006 by Jim Madsen
"Rikki-Tikki-Tavi and the Mystery in the Garden"
Published 2006 by Sterling Publishing, Co.
Illustrations © 2006 by Jim Madsen
"Mowgli's Big Birthday"
© 2007 by Sterling Publishing Co., Inc.
Illustrations © 2007 by Nathan Hale
"Mowgli Knows Best"
© 2007 by Sterling Publishing Co., Inc.
Illustrations © 2007 by Nathan Hale
"The Boy and His Sled Dog"
© 2010 by Sterling Publishing Co., Inc.
Illustrations © 2010 by Nathan Hale
"The Brave Little Seal"
© 2010 by Sterling Publishing Co., Inc.
Illustrations © 2010 by Nathan Hale

ISBN 978-1-4549-0583-7 (hardcover)
ISBN 978-1-4549-0584-4 (paperback)

Distributed in Canada by Sterling Publishing
c/o Canadian Manda Group, 165 Dufferin Street
Toronto, Ontario, Canada M6K 3H6
Distributed in the United Kingdom by GMC Distribution Services
Castle Place, 166 High Street, Lewes, East Sussex, England BN7 1XU
Distributed in Australia by Capricorn Link (Australia) Pty. Ltd.
P.O. Box 704, Windsor, NSW 2756, Australia

For information about custom editions, special sales, and premium and corporate purchases,
please contact Sterling Special Sales at 800-805-5489 or specialsales@sterlingpublishing.com.

Manufactured in China
Lot #:
2  4  6  8  10  9  7  5  3  1
06/13

www.sterlingpublishing.com/kids

# Contents

## CHAPTER ONE

# Rikki-Tikki-Tavi Moves In

One morning,
a very curious little
mongoose said,
"Today I want
to explore.
I want to explore
my burrow!"
So he started to dig.

This little mongoose
was a little *too* curious.
He did not listen
when raindrops started
falling from the sky.
He only dug deeper.
He just *had* to know
how far down he could go!

He did not see
the lightning.
He did not hear
the thunder.

He did not see or hear
anything at all until . . .

*Whish!Whoosh!*
Water poured
into the burrow.

It carried him into the garden—
the garden in front of the house
a little boy
lived in.

"May we keep him, Mama?"
asked the little boy.
"Teddy," Mama said to him,
"you know a mongoose
can cause a lot of trouble."
"Not this one!" said Teddy.
"Not my mongoose,
Rikki-tikki-tavi!"
Teddy carried Rikki
into the house.

Rikki-tikki-tavi had never been
inside a house before.
He was very curious—
a little *too* curious!

He just *had* to know
what was in those sacks.
He just *had* to know
what was under
that plant.

The little boy
chased Rikki around.
Mama's lamps and vases
crashed to the floor.

"Teddy," said Mama,
"that mongoose must go!"
"Please, Mama," Teddy said.
"Give him one more chance."

"Well, all right," said Mama.
"He can stay—for now—
but not in my house.
Go run and play outside."

Rikki and Teddy played
all morning long.
Rikki showed Teddy
how to play
the mongoose way.
They explored the garden.
They dug a big hole
deep in the ground.

"It's time for lunch!"
Mama called.
Teddy told Rikki
to wait for him
in the garden.
"Do not go into
the tall, tall grass,"
said Teddy.

Rikki was very curious.
What could be in
the tall, tall grass?
He just *had* to know!
He tiptoed into it.
Suddenly . . .

. . . out popped a snake!

"Who are *you*?" Snake hissed.

"Who are *you*?" asked Rikki.

"I am Snake," Snake hissed.

"Snake, Master of the Garden."

"No you are not!"
said Rikki.
"Snake, you are not
Master of the Garden!
The garden belongs to me—
to Teddy and me!"

Just then,
Teddy came out
of the house.
"Rikki-tikki-tavi!
Let's play!" Teddy called.

"I have to go," Rikki said.

"Wait," hissed Snake.

"I have an idea."

Rikki knew he should
go to Teddy—
but he was too curious.
He just *had* to know
Snake's idea!

"You think *you* are
Master of the Garden,"
hissed Snake,
"and I think I am.
So, little mongoose,
why don't we race?
Whoever wins will be
the one and only
Master of the Garden."

"A race from where
to where?" Rikki asked.
"From here to there,"
hissed Snake.
Then he took off—
straight for Teddy.

Rikki started after Snake.
Soon they were neck and neck.
Then Rikki passed Snake!
Rikki was so excited,
he forgot to look where he was going.
He forgot the hole
he and Teddy dug that morning . . .
and down he went!

"Ouch," he said. "My paw!"
Rikki quickly got up.
He peeked his head
out of the hole.
*Oh, no!* he thought.
*Snake is winning!*

Rikki knew he did not
have much time.
He jumped out of the hole.
He jumped as high as he could.
He jumped over Snake—

and into Teddy's arms!
Just then, Teddy saw Snake.
"Oh, a snake," said Teddy.
"Snakes are dangerous.
Into the house, Rikki!"

Teddy saw that Rikki
had hurt his paw.
He ran into the house.
"Mama," he said, "Rikki is hurt!"

"Oh, poor little mongoose,"
Mama said, bandaging his paw.
"You are just a little
*too* curious, aren't you?"

"Rikki needs us, Mama,"
Teddy said. "Can't he stay?"
Mama looked down at Rikki.
He snuggled deeper in her arms.
"All right, Teddy," said Mama,
"but I hope he can learn
to be a little less curious!"
*Don't worry, Mama,*
Rikki thought.
*I might never*
*be curious enough*
*to leave this safe home!*

## CHAPTER TWO

# Rikki-Tikki-Tavi and the Mystery in the Garden

Rikki-tikki-tavi loved
to play in the garden
with the little boy, Teddy.
Teddy loved to play
with the little mongoose, too.
He also loved to eat.

"Time for lunch,"
Teddy's mama called.

"Stay here, Rikki," Teddy said.
"Guard the house—
and stay away from
the tall, tall grass.
That is where the snakes are!"

Rikki knew he should listen to Teddy, but Rikki was very curious. A little *too* curious! He just *had* to explore the tall, tall grass.

He had to see what was there.
Soon he saw a
very strange thing—
a creature on a rock.
"Who are you?"
Rikki asked.

"I am a turtle, but I lost
my shell," hissed the creature.
"I will find it!" Rikki said.
Off he went to look.

Rikki looked high and low
for the turtle shell.
Meanwhile, the creature
slipped away.

It was not
a turtle after all!
It was Snake—
and he was heading
for Teddy's house!

Snake was curious, too.
He just *had* to know
what was in Teddy's house.
Snake knew he had to
get Rikki out of the way.
Rikki would never let
a snake in the house.

*That was a good trick*
*I played on the mongoose,*
Snake thought.
*Now, Rikki is busy*
*looking for a turtle shell—*
*and I am free to go inside!*

Snake went into the pantry.
He made a very big mess.
  "This is fun," Snake hissed.
Then he went into the living room.

Snake found Mama's plant.
He curled up in its leaves.
The plant tipped over—
and broke Mama's new lamp.
Mama and Teddy came running.

So did Rikki.
He had not found
the shell that the
creature had lost,

but he had heard
that great big crash.
"I'm coming, Teddy!"
Rikki called.

"Look what Rikki did!"
Mama said to Teddy.
"He didn't!" Teddy said.
"I told him to stay
in the garden."

"Who was it, then?"
asked Mama.
Teddy did not know
what to say.
Neither did Rikki.

"Rikki *must* have
done this," Mama said.
"Now he cannot come
inside the house."
Rikki was very sad.
He wandered away.
Then he heard crying
from the tall, tall grass,
and he forgot he was sad.
He was curious again!

Rikki crept into
the tall, tall grass.
There he saw the
creature again.

"What is wrong?" asked Rikki.

"You have not found my shell yet!"
the creature said. "Won't you help?"
Rikki left to search the grass—
while the creature slipped away.

This time, though, Rikki saw
the creature slip away . . .
and Rikki was very curious.
He just *had* to know
where it was going!

Rikki followed the creature.

First it lost one leg.

Then it lost another.

Then it lost two more!

*This is very strange,*
Rikki thought.

Soon Rikki saw who
that creature *really* was.

"It is not a turtle!" Rikki said.
"It is Snake—and he
is going to the house!"

Snake slipped inside
through a hole in the floor
while Mama stood
at the door, sweeping.

Mama had said Rikki
was not allowed inside,
but the little mongoose
knew he had no choice.
He squeezed into
the hole in the floor.
He had to catch Snake!

Snake was in the pantry.
He was playing with
jars and cans.

"Stop that!" said Rikki.
Snake did not.

*Crash!*

*Smash!*

*Splat!*

They all fell down!

"Get out! Get out!"
Rikki said.

"Catch me if you can,"
hissed Snake.

Rikki chased Snake
around and around.
Rikki ran as fast as he could.
He ran right into Mama!

"Rikki, how could you
make this mess?" she asked.
   "*Achoo!*" sneezed Snake.
   "Look!" said Teddy.
"Rikki did *not* make it.
Snake made it!"

Mama was surprised.
"It was Snake the
whole time!" she said.
Quick as a wink,
she swept Snake out
of the house . . .

. . . and back into
the tall, tall grass—
which Rikki was never
the least bit curious
about ever again.

## CHAPTER THREE

# Mowgli's Big Birthday

Mowgli was excited.
Today was his birthday.
"I am all grown up," he said.
His friends came to celebrate.
Bagheera, the black
panther, was there.
So was Baloo,
the wise brown bear.

"Happy birthday!" said
Bagheera and Baloo.
They loved to tickle Mowgli
to hear the funny sound he makes.

"Do you remember how
you became our cub?"
Father Wolf asked.
Mowgli did not.

"I will tell him,"
growled Baloo.
"No, I will tell him,"
roared Bagheera.

"It was the middle of the night," Father Wolf began. "You were just a tiny cub," Mother Wolf added.

"You escaped from
Shere Khan," said Baloo.
"Who is Shere Khan?"
Mowgli asked.

"We have told you
many times," said Baloo.
"He is a mean, angry
tiger," said Bagheera.

"I'm not afraid of
a tiger," said Mowgli.
"Well, you should be,"
scolded Mother Wolf.

"Tell me more
about the night I
came," Mowgli asked.
"The other wolves
were not very happy,"
said Father Wolf.
"They were afraid because you
are a man-cub, not a wolf."

"I promised to teach you
our ways," said Baloo.
"I vowed to keep you
safe," said Bagheera.

"Safe from what?"
Mowgli asked.
"Hush," said Mother Wolf.
"He's back," said Bagheera.
"Who?" Mowgli asked.

"Run, Mowgli!" Baloo said.

"Why?" Mowgli asked.

Then he heard a low, mean growl.

"Take him to the den,"
Father Wolf told Mother.
"Give me the man-cub,"
Shere Khan demanded.
"He belongs to me!"
"Never!" Bagheera replied.
"We shall see about
that," Shere Khan said.

Shere Khan sent
a message to
the Wolf Council.
"Give me the man-cub,
or I will come after you!"
All the wolves
were worried.
They called a meeting.

While the Wolf Council met,
Mowgli crept up behind.
He wanted to hear what
the wolves had to say.

"The man-cub is
a danger to us all,"
an old wolf said.
"No! He's one of us,"
said Mother Wolf.
"Shere Khan will be
back!" another shouted.
"Mowgli must go at once!"

Mowgli knew that the
old wolf spoke the truth.
To save his family and
all the wolves, he had to go.

"We will go with you,"
said Bagheera.
"Why?" Mowgli asked.
"We love you," said Baloo.

"We will miss you, Mowgli,"
said his wolf brothers.
They licked him on
his hands and his face.

They licked him on his knees
and the bottoms of his feet.
They loved to hear
that funny sound he makes.

"Where are we going?"
Mowgli asked Baloo.
"Someplace safe," said the
wise, old brown bear.
"Where is that?"
Mowgli asked Bagheera.
"Follow me," was all
Bagheera would say.

"I won't leave
until you tell me.
Where are we going?"
Mowgli asked.

"Now, Mowgli," Baloo said slowly, "the first rule of the jungle is this: When Bagheera and I tell you something, you must listen and do just what we say."

"Why should I?"
asked Mowgli.
"Because we say so,"
answered Baloo.
Then he slung Mowgli
over his shoulder.
Bagheera tickled
his feet with his tail.

The three friends went to find
a safe place for Mowgli.
They left the wolf
den far behind.
But sometimes at night
the wolves could still
hear that funny sound
only Mowgli makes.

## CHAPTER FOUR

# Mowgli Knows Best

Mowgli and his friends
Bagheera, the panther, and
Baloo, the bear, had traveled
through the jungle for many weeks.
Bagheera and Baloo
showed Mowgli how to
live safely in the jungle.
But Mowgli did not listen.

"If you see the tiger Shere Khan,
climb a tree!" said Baloo.
"Why should I?" asked Mowgli.
"I would rather stay and fight!"

"If you see Kaa, the rock snake,"
said Bagheera, "run away
as fast as you can!"
"You look funny!" Mowgli laughed.

"Mowgli, stop!" Bagheera said.
"I want to play," said Mowgli.
Baloo and Bagheera
just shook their heads.

"This is your fault," said Baloo.

"You spoil him," growled Bagheera.

"You never let him play!" said Baloo.

"The jungle is not a playground!" Bagheera roared.

Baloo and Bagheera were
so busy shouting, they did
not see Mowgli creep away.

"Where is Mowgli?" asked Baloo.

"He was right here," Bagheera said.

They did not see Mowgli anywhere.

"We must find him," said Baloo.

"Mowgli! Where are you?" they called.

Mowgli didn't hear them, but

Shere Khan, the tiger, and

Kaa, the rock snake, heard them well.

Baloo and Bagheera
crashed through the jungle.
Baloo stopped, "Listen!" he said.
Then Bagheera heard it, too.
"It is the giggle sound that
only Mowgli makes," said Baloo.
"If we can hear it, so can
Shere Khan," worried Bagheera.

Mowgli was with the monkeys,
who laughed and played all day.
He liked them very much.
They liked Mowgli, too.

"There he is!" cried Bagheera.

"Quick, save him!" said Baloo.

"Hold on, Mowgli," they shouted,

"We're coming to rescue you!"

"I don't want to leave!"
Mowgli shook his head.
"I want to stay here and
have fun," he said.

"The monkeys will play
tricks on you," growled Bagheera.
"That's not true!" Mowgli said.
"Stop this, Mowgli!" said Baloo.

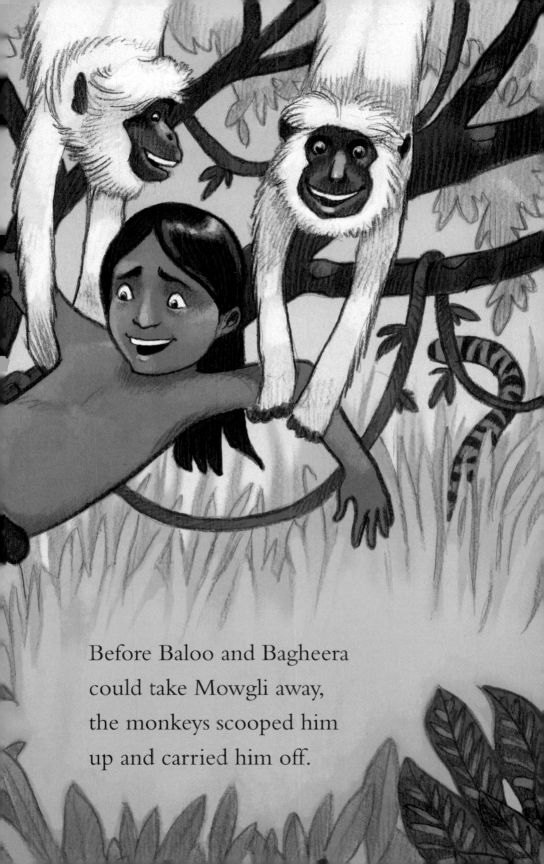

Before Baloo and Bagheera
could take Mowgli away,
the monkeys scooped him
up and carried him off.

Mowgli showed off for the
monkeys all day long.
He did somersaults and cartwheels
while they clapped and laughed.
They never said, "Mowgli, stop!"
When Mowgli was done,
the monkeys were bored.
They looked for something else to do.

The monkeys spotted
Kaa, the rock snake, sleeping
on a rock in the sun.
"Let's play a trick," they said.

While Kaa was fast asleep,
the monkeys laughed
as they tied him into tight knots
and hung him over a tree limb.

"You'll hurt him!" Mowgli told them.
The monkeys just ignored him.
"That's not funny," Mowgli said.
"Yes it is!" they laughed.

Mowgli waited for the monkeys
to go somewhere else to play.
Slowly, gently, he untied the knots,
just as Kaa began to wake.

"What are you doing, man-cub?"
Kaa asked Mowgli with a hiss.
"Untying you," Mowgli said.
"Aren't you afraid?" asked Kaa.
"Nothing scares me," said Mowgli.
"Is that so?" Kaa hissed.

"Run, Mowgli, run!" Baloo cried.
"Let the man-cub go, Kaa,"
Bagheera snarled angrily.

"Wait!" shouted Mowgli,
"He is my friend!"
"What?" asked Bagheera.
"Who?" asked Baloo.
"Me!" hissed Kaa with an evil smile.

Baloo and Bagheera could
not believe their ears.

"Kaa is no one's friend," Baloo said.

"He is, too!" Mowgli said.

"He is not!" Bagheera growled.

While they argued, Kaa tightened
his coils around Mowgli and smiled.

"At last! The man-cub is mine!"
Shere Khan the tiger roared.
He leaped from the bushes,
heading straight for the boy.

"Give me the man-cub, Kaa!"
Shere Khan roared.

"Never!" hissed Kaa, "He's mine!"

"Leave us!" growled Baloo.

"Now!" Bagheera roared.

"Let me fight, too!" cried Mowgli,
"You see? You are outnumbered.
"Four of us against you!" hissed Kaa.

Shere Khan looked from one
enemy to the other.
"I'll be back," he growled, and
slouched off into the jungle.

"Let the man-cub go," growled Baloo.

"Why should I?" Kaa hissed back.

"We say so," roared Bagheera.

Slowly Kaa unwound his coils.

"I hope you learned your lesson
this time," Baloo began to say.
"Where is he?" asked Bagheera.
Then they heard the sound
that only Mowgli makes.
They looked at each other.
They started to run.
"Here we go again!"

## CHAPTER FIVE

# The Boy and His Sled Dog

In a cold and snowy
faraway place, there lived
a little Inuit boy
named Quiquern.
Quiquern wanted to drive
a sled so he could hunt
and fish like the older
boys in his village.

"I want to come with you,"
Quiquern said to a group of boys.
"I can hunt and fish as well as you!"
The boys just laughed.

"Father, I want to hunt and fish!"
said Quiquern.
"Son," his father said.
"You have much to learn if you
want to become a great hunter.
Here, this is for you."

His father handed Quiquern
a small puppy and a sled,
just the right size for a boy.
Quiquern's face lit up.

"I will name him Dog!"
said Quiquern.
"I will take care of him.
I will teach him to be the
best sled dog in the village."

Quiquern put the puppy on the sled
and gave him a ride.
Quinquern wanted Dog to know
just what to do when it was his turn
to pull the sled.

Quiquern and Dog
played hide-and-seek so Dog
would learn to hunt.

They played fetch,
so Dog would learn to fish.
At last, Dog was ready!
He could hunt and fish,
and he could pull Quiquern's sled.

"Father, watch me!" Quiquern called.
"Go, Dog, go!" he shouted.
Dog began to run.
Dog and the sled went one way.
Quiquern went the other!
"Some great hunter!" the
older boys laughed.

Soon after, it began to snow.
At first, snowflakes drifted
down slowly from the sky.
Then the flakes came faster
and thicker until the whole
village was covered in a
frozen white blanket of snow.

There was more snow than
the villagers had ever seen.
The snow covered all the
houses and sleds.

The villagers tried to free their sleds
from the heavy ice and snow.
"Pull!" they shouted to the dogs.
"Push!" they yelled at each other.

For many days, they could not
move the sleds and could not
get out on the ice to fish.
The villagers were very hungry.

"I can fish, Father!" Quiquern said.
"My sled is light.
The snow can't stop me."
"It is too far for you and Dog
to go alone," Father said.
"Let me try, Father, or everyone in
the village will starve,"
begged Quiquern.

Quiquern and Dog pushed
through the snow.
They needed to get to the holes
in the ice where they could fish.
When they were halfway there,
another snowstorm began.
Quiquern and Dog spent a
cold night in a cave.
But they were not afraid.
They had each other.

The next morning,
Quiquern and Dog woke up.
The air was filled with
blinding snow.
Quiquern did not know
which way to go!
Just then, they both heard
a low, scary growl.

"Wolf!" shouted Quiquern.
The hairs on Dog's back
stood up on end.
Dog bared his teeth
and gave a long, deep growl.
"Dog! No! Stay here!"
Quiquern cried out.

The wolf bared his teeth,
but Dog did not budge.
Dog stared at the wolf
for a long, long time
until the wolf finally backed
down and turned away.

Meanwhile, the sun came out
and the snow stopped falling.
Quiquern was able to see the path
to the fishing holes in the ice.
"Run, Dog!" Quiquern shouted
as he jumped onto the sled.
Before long, Quiquern and Dog
were at the fishing holes.

Quiquern dropped his fishing
line down into a hole
the way he had seen his
father and the older boys do.

After a short time, Quiquern
felt a tug on his fishing line.
"A fish!" Quiquern called out.
The fish tugged harder ...
and harder! It pulled
and pulled against Quiquern's line.
"Help me, Dog!" Quiquern cried.

Quiquern and Dog
tugged and pulled and
pulled and tugged until …
"We've got him!" Quiquern
shouted with glee.
The big fish flopped
onto the ice with a
great big *plop*!

Quiquern and Dog
returned to the village with a
fish big enough to feed everyone.
"Hurray for Quiquern,"
the villagers shouted.
Quiquern and Dog were heroes!
And from that day on, Quiquern was
always asked to join the hunting party.

## CHAPTER SIX

# The Brave Little Seal

Once upon a time,
there was a place
called Seal Haven,
where all the Arctic seals lived.
One spring, a special
seal pup was born.
His name was Kotick.

From the time he was born,
Kotick knew he was special.
He could not wait to do
everything the grown-up seals did.

He was the first seal pup
to crawl and swim.
He could dive the
deepest in the sea.
He was the first
to catch a fish.
And he was always
first to the cliff top.

One day, Kotick went
exploring by himself.
That's when he saw
the seal hunters!

"Look! A white seal!" a hunter shouted.
"He's bad luck! Catch him!"
Kotick raced into the sea.
He swam as fast and as far as he could.

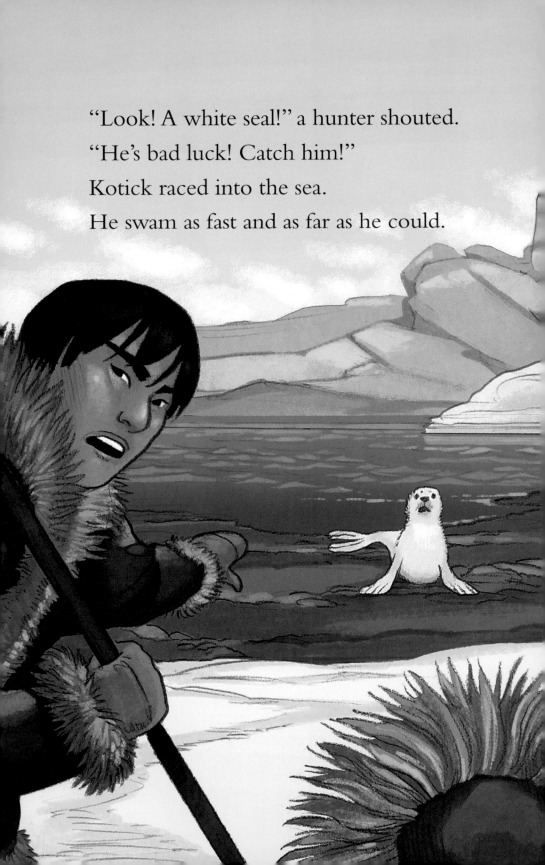

Kotick swam and swam.
After many miles,
he came up for air
and scrambled onto
an icy bank. There were
no seals in sight.
Kotick saw a crowd of
giant, sleepy walruses.

"Wake up! Wake up!"
shouted Kotick.
"Who are you to talk to me?"
asked the biggest walrus of all.
"The seals need help!"
Kotick explained. "They
need a place safe from the hunters."

"There is no such place,"
the walrus grunted.
"Go back to Seal Haven,
and don't bother us again!"

Kotick did not know what to do.
"Ask Wise Old Seal
on Old Seal Rock,"
said a seagull as she flew by.

Kotick swam over sharp rocks.
He swam through terrible waves.
He swam until at last he
came to Old Seal Rock.

"Wise Old Seal," Kotick said.
"Where can I find a land
where the seals will be safe?"
Wise Old Seal thought a moment.

"Kotick, you are very special,"
said Wise Old Seal.
"There has never been a white
seal born on our beaches before.
You were sent to us to save
the seals from the hunters.
Find the sea cow. She will
show you where to go."

Kotick slipped back into the sea.
"Where can I find the sea cow?"
Kotick asked the polar bear,
the whale, the shark, and the fish.
"Swim north," they told him.
"Swim as far as you can go."

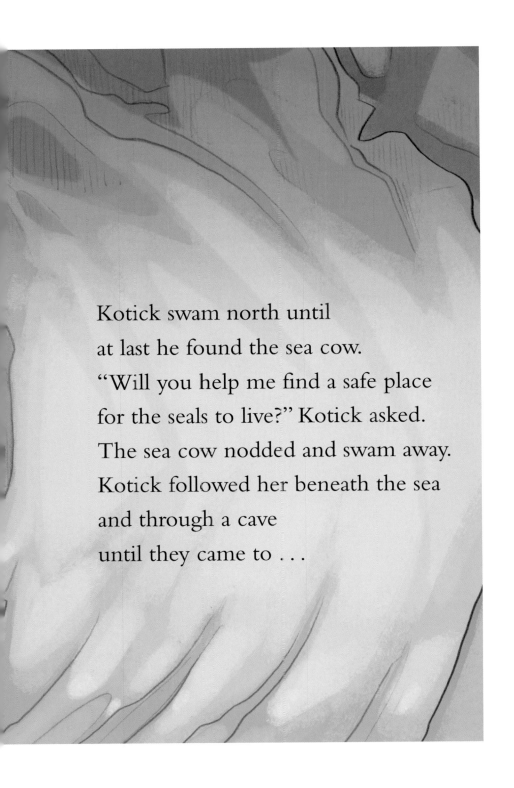

Kotick swam north until
at last he found the sea cow.
"Will you help me find a safe place
for the seals to live?" Kotick asked.
The sea cow nodded and swam away.
Kotick followed her beneath the sea
and through a cave
until they came to . . .

. . . a beautiful beach with
nothing but sea cows!
There were smooth rock piles
where baby seals could be born.
There were sandy playgrounds
where young seals could have fun.
And there were warm grassy
spots where the seals could nap.

"There are no hunters here,"
Kotick said.
"This is the perfect place!"
Then Kotick swam all the way back
to Seal Haven to tell the others.

Kotick returned to
Seal Haven as fast
as he could swim.
But hunters were on their
way to Seal Haven, too!

Danger was getting
closer and closer.
Kotick shouted to warn
the other seals, but they
laughed and ignored him.

Then Wise Old Seal swam up.
"I am the last of the old and wise.
In my early days, there was a story
often told that one day a white seal
would come and lead the seals
to a quiet place.
That day has come.
We must follow Kotick if we hope
to survive."

Just then, the hunters arrived.

"What do we do?" the seals cried.

"Follow me!" Kotick shouted.

Kotick led the seals into the water.

They dived deep beneath the sea.

They swam through the underwater cave,

until they arrived at . . .

. . . every seal's paradise!

"We're safe, now!" Kotick said.

"Thanks to Kotick," shouted one seal.

"Hurray for Kotick!" shouted another
and another until Kotick's
name rang out across the beach.
From that day forward, Kotick was
known as the bravest seal of all.